Don't you dare, Dragon!

by
Annie Kubler

Child's Play (International) Ltd
Swindon   Auburn ME   Sydney
© 2006 Child's Play (International) Ltd   Printed in China
ISBN 978-1-84643-045-9
5 7 9 10 8 6
www.childs-play.com

I'm going ice-skating!

You're a disaster, Dragon!

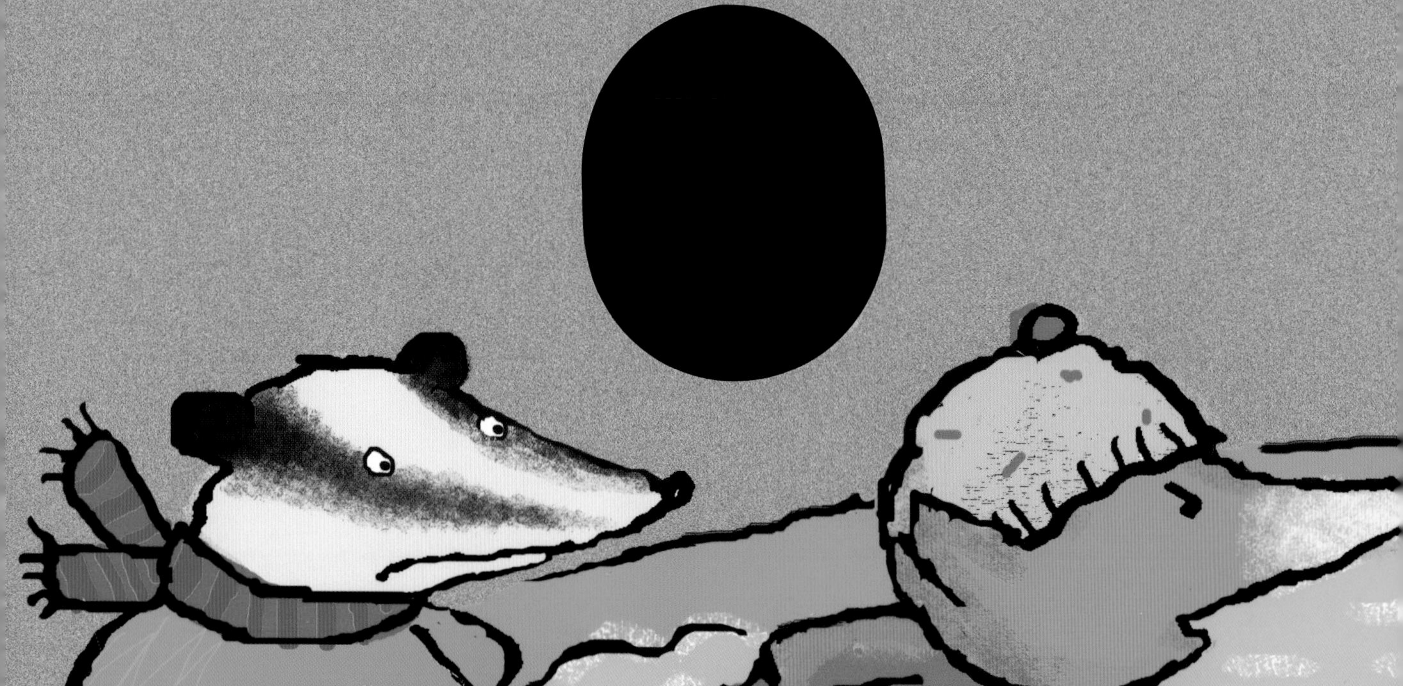

You melted all the ice!

I'm sorry! I didn't mean to.

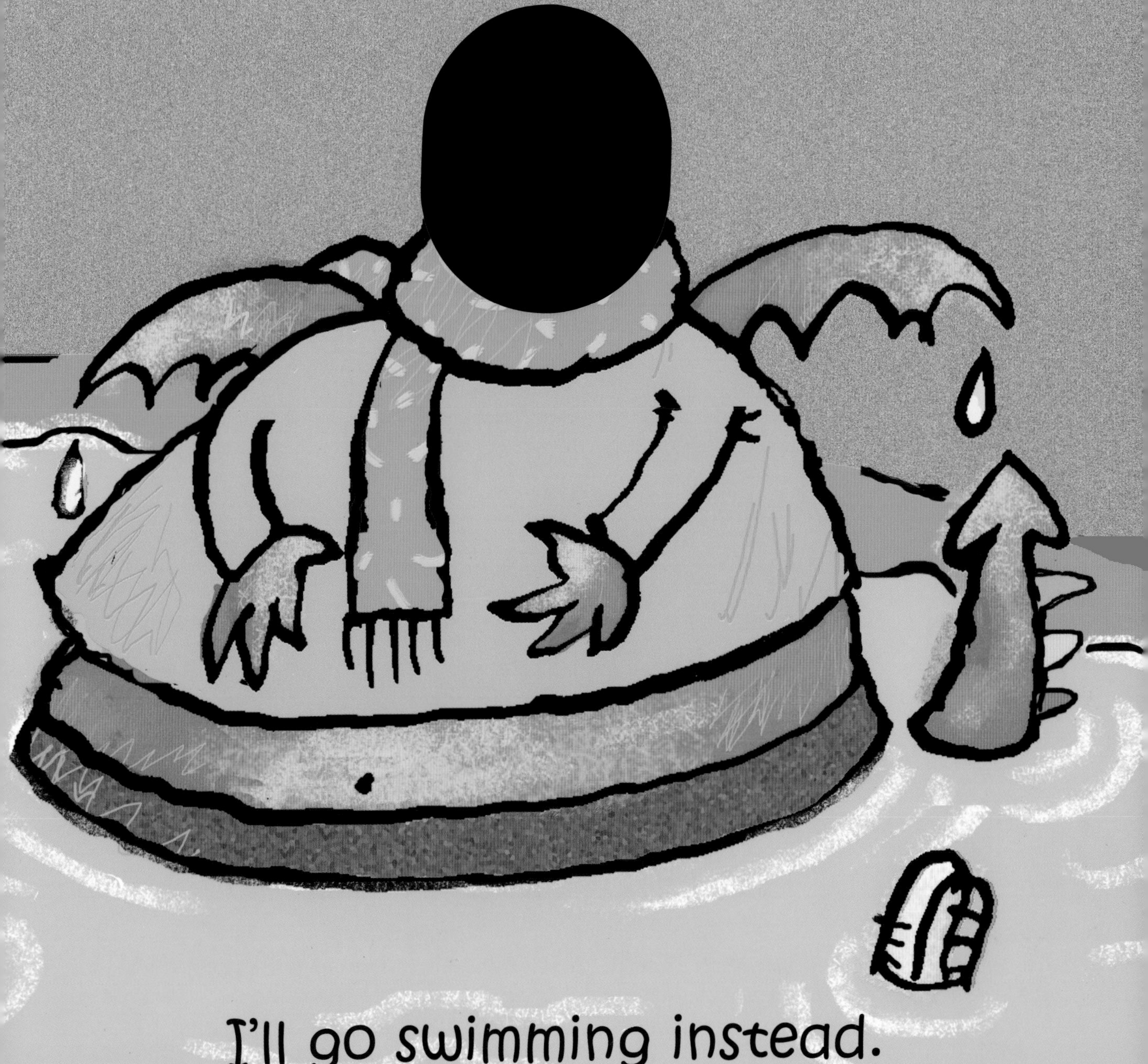

I'll go swimming instead.

Don't you dare, Dragon!

I'm sorry! I didn't mean to.

I'll go for an ice-cream instead.

Don't you dare, Dragon!

I'm sorry! I didn't mean to.

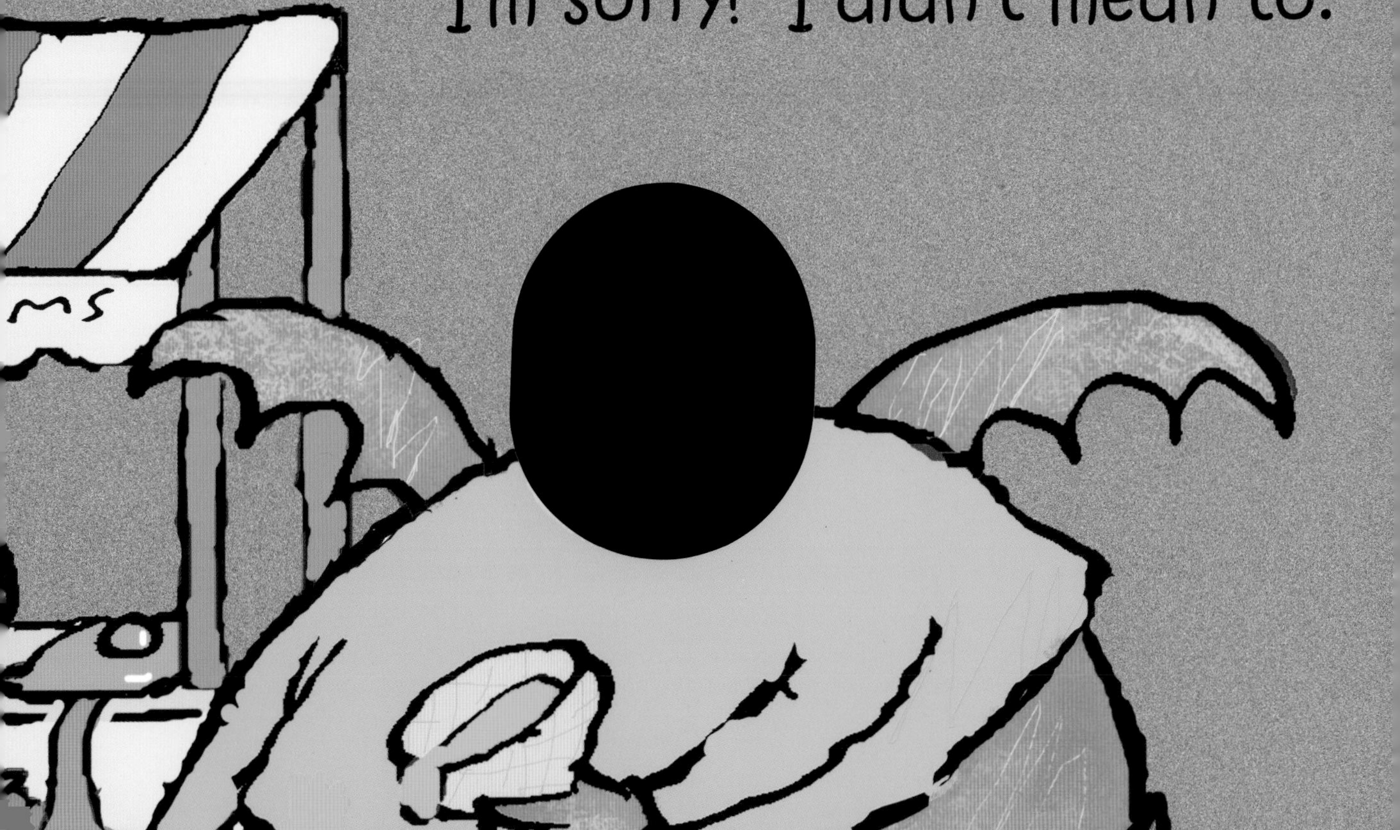

I'll go to the play area instead.

Don't you dare, Dragon!

You're a disgrace, Dragon!

You burned holes in the castle.

I'm sorry! I didn't mean to.

I'll go somewhere else to play.

No one loves me!

Oh **YES**! It's Dragon! Come over here

Who, me? Really?

Please light the candles on our cake!
And enjoy the party!